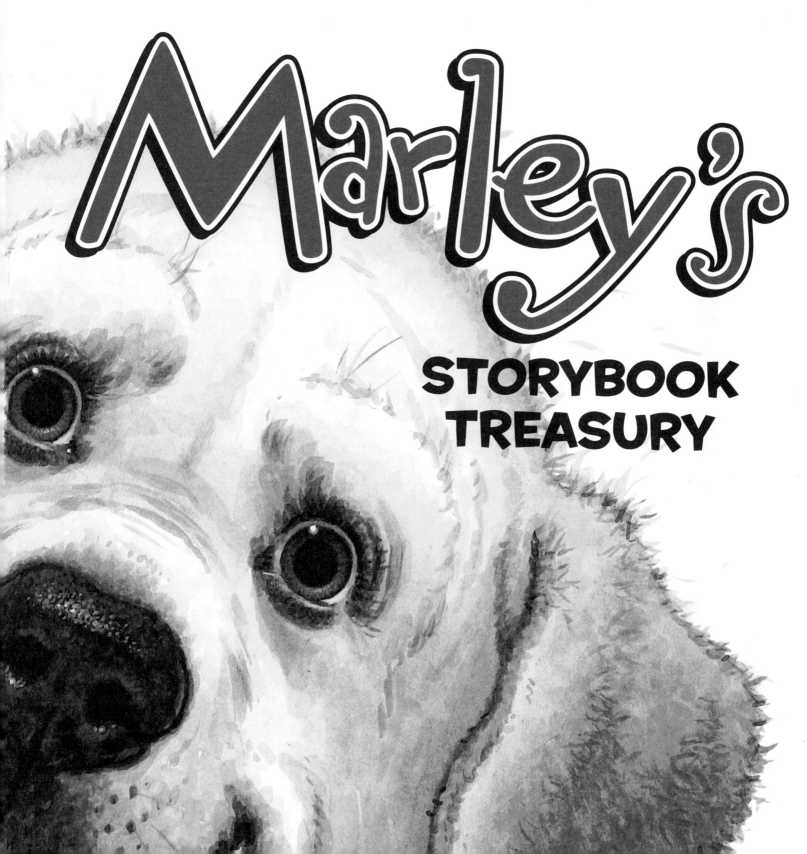

Marley's

STORYBOOK TREASURY

This Treasury Belongs To:

Marley's
STORYBOOK
TREASURY

Based on the bestselling books by John Grogan

Cover art by Richard Cowdrey

HARPER
An Imprint of HarperCollins Publishers

Contents

Marley woke up his family

one morning

with a "ruff-ruff-ruff!"

"Bad dog, Marley," said Daddy.

"It's too soon to wake up."

Cassie and Baby Louie
were ready to play.
Cassie jumped out of bed.
But Baby Louie couldn't get out
of his crib.

Marley stared at the crib.

"I'll get you out of that cage!"

he thought.

Marley jumped into the crib.

Then he hung Baby Louie over the rail.

"Bad dog, Marley!" yelled Mommy.

"Baby Louie could get hurt!"

Daddy made breakfast.

He flipped a pancake.

Up flew the pancake.

Up jumped Marley.

He fetched the pancake in midair.

"Bad dog, Marley!" yelled Daddy.

"Run and get dressed
so we can go to the playground,"
Mommy said to Cassie.

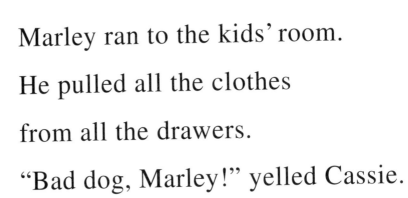

Marley ran to the kids' room.

He pulled all the clothes

from all the drawers.

"Bad dog, Marley!" yelled Cassie.

Mommy put Marley outside.

"We need a break," she said.

Marley howled.

It was a sad sound.

"Maybe they don't love me now,"
he thought.

Marley began to dig.

He dug until he could slip

under the fence.

"Why did he run away?" asked Cassie.

"Doesn't he know we love him?"

Mommy hugged Cassie.

"We'll find him," she said.

"We'll tell him we love him."

Marley was still running.

He missed his family.

His paws hurt from digging.

Suddenly, a wonderful smell

stopped Marley in his tracks.

It smelled better than dog chow,

better than a bone,

better than Baby Louie's sticky face.

"Well, hello there,"

said the man inside the shop.

"Welcome to my bakery."

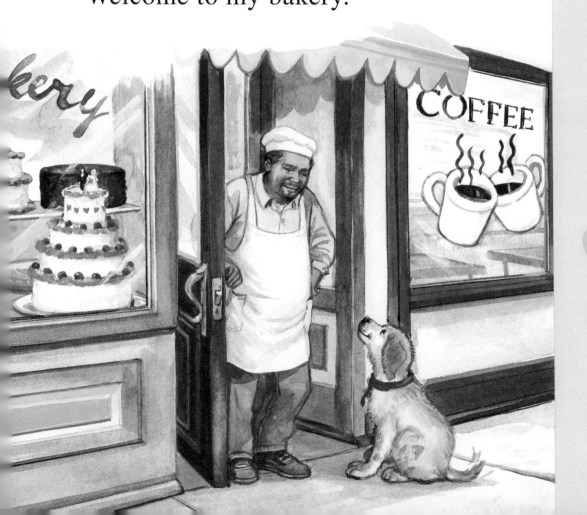

Marley licked the baker's face all over.

"My new home!" he thought.

The baker laughed.

"Good dog," he said.

"I had a dog like you once."

The baker saw Marley's dog tag.
He knew this dog had run away.
"I'll call your owners as soon as
I take these cookies
out of the oven," said the baker.

"Be a good dog and
guard the cookies,"
the baker said to Marley.
Then he went to call
Marley's family.

26

Marley stared at the cookies.

He sniffed at the cakes.

Everything smelled so good!

He started sniffing everything.

Marley sniffed a bag of flour.

Achoo! Marley sneezed.

He jumped and bumped into the table.

Flour, cakes, and cookies

went everywhere.

Then the baker came back.

"My cookies! My cakes!"

yelled the baker.

"And there was no answer

at your house!"

Marley gently set a cookie
at the baker's feet.

The baker scratched Marley's ears.

"You didn't mean to make a mess,"

he said kindly.

Just then, Marley's family ran by.

They'd looked all over for Marley.

"Look at that mess!" said Mommy.

Suddenly, they all stopped.

They knew what that meant.

"Marley!" they shouted.

Mommy, Daddy, Cassie,
and Baby Louie ran inside the bakery
and found their dog at last.
"We love you even if we yell,"
Mommy said.

"We love you even if you

make a mess of our house,"

said Daddy.

"And of my bakery!" said the baker.

Everyone helped the baker clean up.

Marley wagged his tail so hard

he knocked over a chair.

He wanted to help, too.

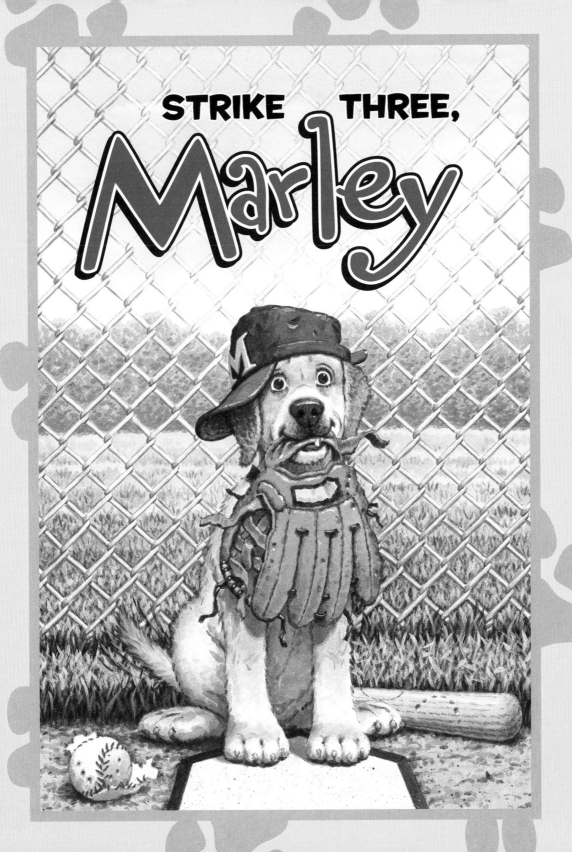

It was spring, and Cassie was going
to her first baseball game.
"Come on, Marley,"
said Daddy.
"You can come, too!"

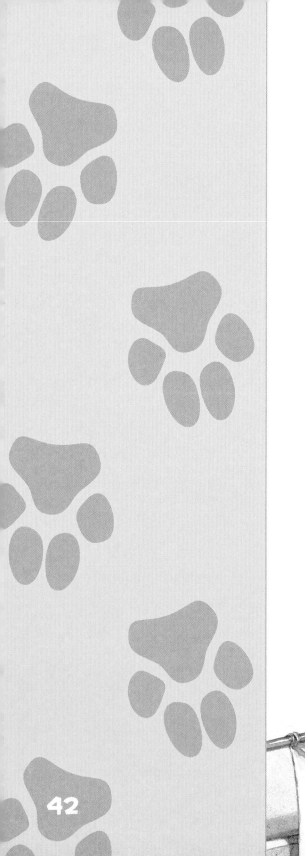

Cassie and Daddy went
to the baseball field.
They found a place to sit,
and then Daddy told Cassie
the rules.
"The pitcher throws the ball,"
Daddy said.
"The batter swings the bat.
If he misses the ball,
it is called a strike.
Three strikes means he's out."

GO
HOME TEAM

Daddy looked hard at Marley.

"Your rules are simple,"

he told him.

"Sit. Stay. Got it?"

"Ruff!" Marley barked.

Cassie laughed.

"If Marley messes up,

we'll call a strike on him!"

The game began.

The pitcher threw the ball.

It went way over the batter's head.

47

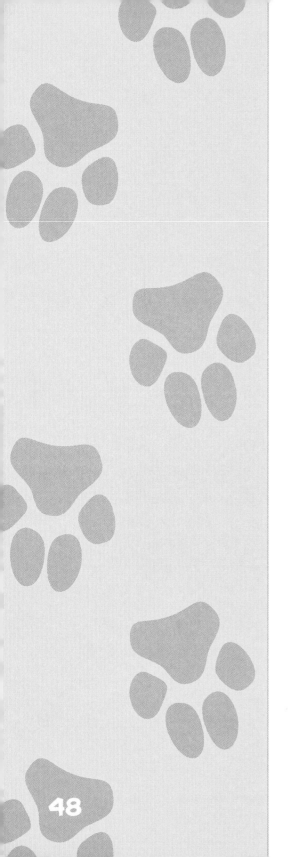

Marley tugged at his leash.

"Sit, Marley," said Daddy.

"That was a wild pitch,"
said Daddy.

"The pitcher must be nervous."

The next pitch went low.

It landed at the batter's feet.

Marley jumped up and down.

"Stay, Marley," Daddy warned.

The pitcher threw the ball again.
This time, the batter hit it
way out over the field.

"They're playing Fetch.

That's my favorite game.

I want to play, too," thought Marley.

Suddenly, Marley broke free

and ran onto the field.

"Sit, Marley! Stay!" yelled Daddy.

Marley did not sit.

He did not stay.

Marley kept his eyes on the ball

and ran as fast as he could.

53

Marley knocked over

the second baseman,

but he didn't stop.

The outfielder dove at Marley
but still Marley didn't stop.

He didn't stop
until he caught that ball!

Then Marley began
to dig like crazy.
The pitcher laughed.
"Sometimes I want
to bury the ball, too," he said.

Daddy and Cassie

chased Marley.

Marley ran away from them.

"Strike one, Marley!" Daddy yelled.

Marley ran to the batter's box

and grabbed the bat in his teeth.

Marley tugged.

The batter tugged back.

Marley tugged harder,

and the batter fell down.

"Strike two, Marley," said Daddy.

Then Marley ran to home base
and grabbed it in his teeth.
"He's stealing home!"
yelled the catcher.

The umpire was mad.

"Uh-oh," said Cassie.

"Strike three, Marley!"

"You're out of the game!"

the umpire yelled.

Marley dropped the base

and stuck out his paw

to shake hands with the umpire.

Daddy grabbed Marley's leash.

By now, everyone was laughing,

even the umpire.

"Sorry," Daddy said to the umpire.

"I guess Marley's not cut out for

the major leagues."

Daddy and Cassie sat down again.

"What did I tell you, Marley?"

said Daddy.

"Sit. Stay.

Is that too much to ask of a dog?"

"Marley didn't sit or stay,"

said Cassie.

"But he did fetch

and shake hands."

Daddy smiled.

"I guess you're right," he said.

"He's a pretty good player,

for a dog."

When the game ended,

the pitcher gave Cassie the ball.

"Thanks to your dog,

I relaxed and pitched my

best game ever!" he said.

Daddy and Cassie hugged Marley.
"We're glad you're on our team,
Marley," said Cassie.

Marley

THANKS, MOM AND DAD!

It was Mommy and Daddy's anniversary, and Cassie and
Baby Louie wanted to help celebrate. But how?

"It has to be special," Cassie said. "And fun, and . . ."
Suddenly her stomach rumbled. "I know!" she cried. "Let's take
them to their favorite Mexican restaurant for lunch!"

Baby Louie clapped his hands. "Me wuv taco!"

73

Soon the family was set to go. Everyone except Marley, that is.

"Are you sure we shouldn't take him with us?" Daddy asked Mommy. "The restaurant allows pets if we sit in the garden."

Marley's ears perked up. He stared at Mommy and whimpered. *"Pleeaaaasse?"* he seemed to say.

Mommy softened. "Do you *promise* to be on your best puppy behavior?" she asked the eager dog.

"WOOF!" Marley replied.

As they walked to the restaurant, it was clear that Marley would have a tough time keeping his promise. After all, it was a great day for a game of Frisbee . . .

. . . and for flying kites . . .

. . . and for giving Mommy
and Daddy something special.

Finally they arrived at the restaurant. Cassie asked for nachos. Daddy ordered a burrito for himself and a taco for Baby Louie. And Mommy said she'd have a fajita.

"Woof!" Marley barked.

"Marley wants to order, too," Cassie told the waiter.

"Sorry, Marley," Daddy said. "It's dog food for you."

When a mariachi band began to play,
Mommy glanced at Marley. She knew how
he loved to mambo. But Marley didn't
even twitch.

"I guess he really *is* trying to be
good," Mommy said, surprised.

Minutes later, a waiter delivered two steaming plates of food to the next table. Daddy noticed Marley sniffing in the direction of the food. "Don't even think about it," Daddy said.

Marley tried to sit still, but the yummy scent was too much for him to bear. He had to check it out!

Mommy was horrified. "*This* is why
Marley should never come to a restaurant!"

"And *this*!" Mommy added.

"And THAT!" she cried. "Marley, no!"

It looked as if Mommy and Daddy's anniversary lunch was totally ruined. Or was it?

92

Cassie had an idea. "I know!
Let's go to your second favorite
place for lunch," she said. "I hope
you're still hungry."

93

Everybody was—especially Marley!

Marley

MESSY DOG

Mommy was painting the walls
of Cassie's room.

Mommy looked at the new paint
and smiled.

"Cassie is going to love this,"
she said.

Rrrrring!

Mommy went to answer the phone.

Mommy had put Marley in the garage
so he wouldn't get into trouble.
But Marley was good at opening doors.

Marley poked his head
into Cassie's room.
Then he poked his head
into the paint can.

"I can help," Marley thought.

He dipped his tail into the paint.

Then Marley wagged his tail.

"Good job!" Marley thought.

"Cassie is going to love this!"

107

Uh-oh!

Marley tipped over the paint can.

Paint spilled all over.

"No problem," thought Marley.

"I'll just cover it up."

But even Marley could see

his fix didn't work.

Marley heard Mommy's footsteps.

He ran and hid in the tub.

"I can finish painting now,"
said Mommy.

"I can't wait to show Cassie."

Mommy stopped in her tracks.

"Oh, no!" she yelled.

"This mess has Marley
written all over it!"

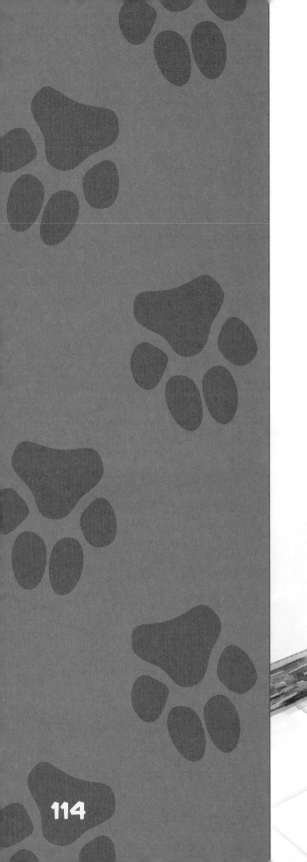

Mommy followed Marley's tracks
down the hall.
"Marley!" she yelled.

The tracks went into the bathroom.

So did Mommy.

"I know you're in there, Marley!"

she shouted.

Mommy looked in the tub.

Marley was not there.

Mommy was mad!

"You can run, Marley," she yelled,

"but you can't hide!"

Marley could hear Mommy yelling.

He jumped into a pile of leaves
and hid.

"Get that messy dog!"

Mommy yelled.

Daddy poked at the leaf pile.

"Any purple dogs in there?"

The leaf pile suddenly exploded!

"Stop, Marley!" Cassie yelled.

But Marley didn't stop.

He ran and tried to hide in a puddle.

"You are one messy dog, Marley,"
Daddy said.

"Let's clean him up,"
said Mommy.

"Oh, MESSY DOG, Marley!"

said Cassie.

They all went to look

at Cassie's room.

"Don't worry, Cassie," said Mommy.

"I'll paint it again,

with no help from Marley."

"I love it just the way it is!"

Cassie said.

"I knew she would," thought Marley.

"Ruff-ruff!"

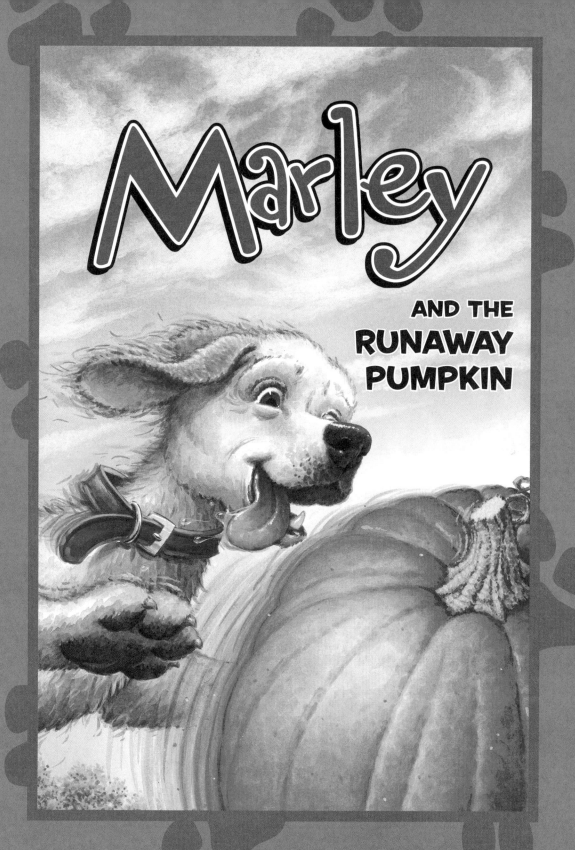

Late one day in fall,

Daddy, Cassie, and Baby Louie

went out to the garden

to look at their pumpkin.

All summer and fall,

the family tended the pumpkin.

They gave it food and water,

sun and shade,

and plenty of room to grow.

All summer and fall,

they kept their big puppy, Marley,

out of the garden.

Now the pumpkin was round.

It was orange.

And it was very, very big.

"Will it win a prize?"

Cassie asked.

Daddy nodded proudly.

"We might even win a blue ribbon,"

he said.

"But first, we have to get

the pumpkin to the fair."

The next day,

Daddy snipped the pumpkin

from the vine.

Mommy helped Daddy roll the pumpkin
to the truck.

Marley batted at the pumpkin.

"That's not a ball, Marley,"
said Mommy.

"That's our blue-ribbon pumpkin!"

137

Daddy tied Marley up.

"Sorry, Marley," he said,

"but we can't let you mess up

our blue-ribbon pumpkin."

Then Daddy and Mommy tried
to lift the pumpkin onto the truck.
"It's too big to lift," said Mommy.
"What will we do?" asked Cassie.

Daddy went inside and came back
with the ironing board.

"This can be a ramp," he said.

Cassie helped Mommy and Daddy
roll the pumpkin up the ramp.

At last, the pumpkin was ready
to go to the fair.

Everybody got behind the pumpkin
so Mommy could take a picture.

"Say blue ribbon!" said Mommy.

141

Marley wanted to be in the picture.

He tugged at his leash.

Marley broke free

and ran toward the truck.

"No, Marley!" cried Mommy.

Marley made a giant leap,
and landed right on top of
the pumpkin.

The pumpkin rolled out
from under Marley.

The pumpkin rolled out of the truck

and down the ramp,

and then it kept on rolling.

Marley ran after the pumpkin.

Daddy ran after Marley.

Cassie ran after Daddy,

and Baby Louie sat down and cried.

The pumpkin crashed
into the trash cans,
but it didn't slow down.

It bounced onto a scooter,

but it didn't slow down.

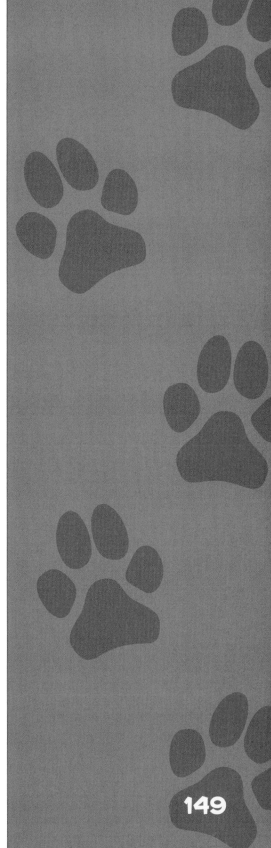

Then the pumpkin rolled up
behind the mailman.

"Look out for the pumpkin!"
yelled Cassie.

The mailman jumped out of the way.

"I almost lost my letters,"

said the mailman.

"Look out for Marley!"

yelled Daddy.

But it was too late.

Marley ran into the mailman.

Down went the mailman.

Over went Marley.

Crash went the pumpkin

at the bottom of the hill.

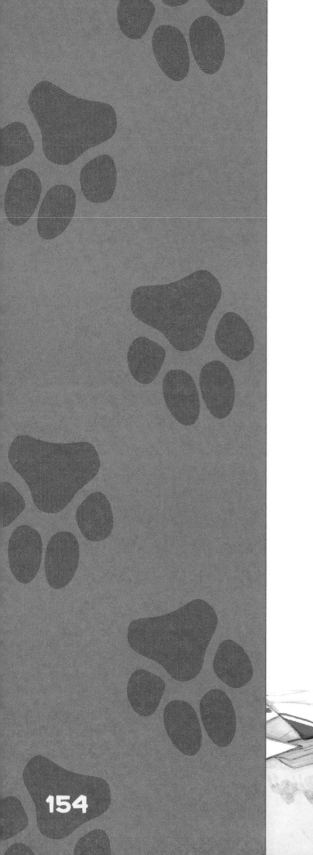

"This is awful," said Cassie.

Mommy gave her a hug.

"When life gives you lemons,

make lemonade," she said.

"And when life gives you

a smashed pumpkin, make pie."

Back at home,

Cassie helped Mommy and Daddy

bake pie.

Lots and lots of pie.

The pie was so good

it won first prize at the fair.

"It was a blue-ribbon pumpkin after all," Cassie said.

And best of all,

there was plenty of pie to share.

SNOW DOG
Marley

Winter had arrived.

Cassie, Baby Louie,

and their big puppy, Marley,

looked out the window.

Snow fell all around.

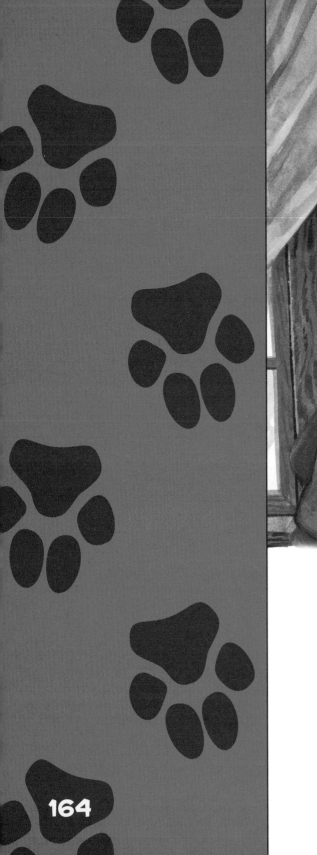

"Have you ever seen so much snow?"

Cassie asked Daddy.

Daddy smiled.

"Never quite this much," he said.

Marley ran to the door and barked.

"Marley wants to play in the snow!"

said Cassie.

165

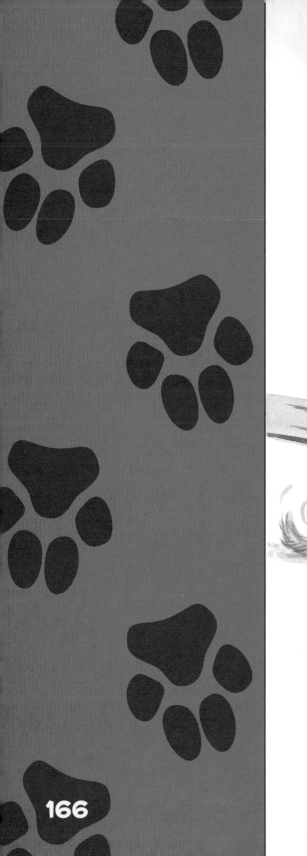

Daddy grabbed a shovel.

"Okay, Marley," he said.

"But before we play,

we need to work."

Everyone put on coats, hats,
mittens, and scarves.
Then they went outside.

Daddy shoveled the walkway.

Marley shoveled, too.

Daddy was surprised.

"Thanks, Marley," said Daddy.

Cassie and Baby Louie
made a snowman.
"Don't eat the carrot nose,"
Cassie said to Marley.

Marley didn't eat the carrot.

Cassie was amazed.

"Good dog, Marley," said Cassie.

Mommy called the family in for lunch.

"Please get the snow

off your boots," she told them.

Marley waited while Mommy

dried his paws.

"Marley's being so good today,"
said Mommy.

"I wonder if it's really our dog
under all that fluff," she joked.

After lunch, it was time to take

soup to a sick friend.

Mommy poured some soup into a pot.

She left the rest of the soup

to cool.

Then everyone went outside,

and Mommy put the pot on the sled.

175

Daddy began to pull the rope.

Marley pulled, too.

"Marley's a snow dog!" said Cassie.

"He rescues people in the snow!"

Daddy let go of the rope.

Mommy frowned.

"Is it a good idea

to let Marley pull the sled?"

"You heard Cassie," said Daddy.

"Marley's a snow dog!"

Mommy smiled.

Everyone held hands

so that nobody would slip and fall.

Marley followed, pulling the sled.

Marley was doing a good job.

The soup pot was still standing,

and he hadn't spilled a drop.

Then Marley saw a kid

throw a snowball.

"Catch that ball!" thought Marley.

Marley started to run.

"Catch that soup!" yelled Mommy.

Marley dove through a snowdrift.

He lurched, he lunged, he leaped. . . .

Marley caught the snowball
in his teeth!

Daddy clapped wildly.

"Good catch!" said Daddy.

Mommy glared at Daddy.

"Bad snow dog," she said.

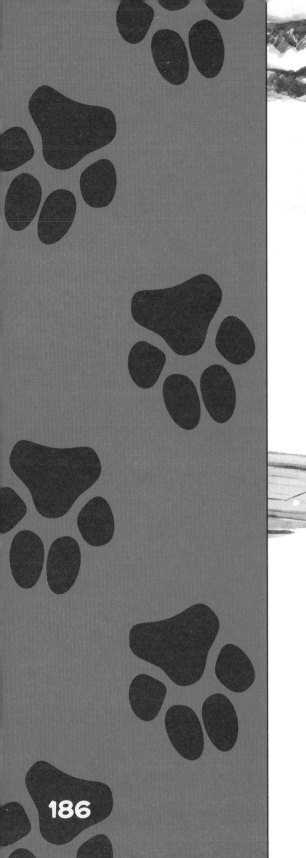

Cassie ran to the sled.

The pot was still on it.

"The soup is safe!" cried Cassie.

"Amazing!" said Daddy.

"Marley didn't spill a drop!"

The family delivered the soup.

Then they walked home.

Marley ran ahead.

"Marley is a snow dog, after all,"
said Mommy.

"But he's still our Marley!"

said Cassie.